The GOLDEN BRACELET

The GOLDEN BRACELET

retold by David Kherdian

illustrated by Nonny Hogrogian

Holiday House/New York

Author's Note

The Golden Bracelet is an old Armenian tale, which has been handed down in many different versions. I've always liked it because it emphasizes the importance of craft and common sense in negotiating the pitfalls of life. In other words, it is not enough to be intelligent, talented, or wealthy—one must be able to *do!*

Text copyright © 1998 by David Kherdian
Illustrations copyright © 1998 by Nonny H. Kherdian
ALL RIGHTS RESERVED
Printed in the United States of America
FIRST EDITION
Library of Congress Cataloging-in-Publication Data
Kherdian, David.
The golden bracelet / by David Kherdian; illustrated by Nonny
Hogrogian — 1st ed.
p. cm.
Summary: In order to win the hand of his love, indolent Prince
Haig learns to weave beautiful golden cloth, a craft that later
saves his life.
ISBN 0-8234-1362-4
[1. Folklore—Armenia.] I. Hogrogian, Nonny, ill. II. Title.
PZ8.1.K553Go 1998
398.2'09566'202[E]—DC20   95-25051
                                             CIP
                                             AC

FOR GLO AND LEO WITH LOVE

There lived long ago, in the ancient land of Armenia, a young, carefree prince by the name of Haig.

Prince Haig was the only child of the king and queen, and now that he had come of age, they were anxious to marry him to someone of royal blood. But Haig was not interested in marrying. He wanted only to hunt with Vartan, who was his faithful servant and dearest friend.

Each morning they arose with the sun, and after readying their equipment, they would mount their steeds and ride out. They were happiest when they were in each other's company, embarked on new adventures that took them into strange and interesting territories.

Now, at this time, there lived in Armenia an evil sorcerer by the name of Zilnago. Through his witchcraft he had turned many of the finest young men in the country into slaves whose labors were making him a rich man. Zilnago had long envied Haig from a distance. The young prince's spirited behavior rankled the old sorcerer, and he was determined to put a stop to Haig's freedom one day. As he continued with his evil design, more and more of the healthiest and strongest males of that place began to disappear.

But of course these concerns were outside the cares of Haig and Vartan, as they rode across the countryside, laughing, singing, and harmlessly bantering. One afternoon they came to the village fountain of a town they had not seen before.

When Haig dismounted and approached the fountain, he was met by a fair maiden carrying a jug. "May I have a drink?" he said, motioning to her jug.

Without answering, the maiden began filling the jug. As Haig studied her movements, he was overtaken by her beauty and her grace. By the time their eyes met, Haig had already fallen in love. Before he was able to notice the blush on her cheeks, she turned from the well and began to walk away.

But Haig called after her, saying, "I failed to ask you your name."

"And I yours," the maiden replied. "I am Anahid, the daughter of the shepherd Aram."

"This is Prince Haig," Vartan interrupted, "the son of our great king."

Haig was upset with his friend, fearing that he had frightened the maiden, but she gave no indication of being disturbed, nor for that matter did she seem surprised.

"The king and queen have been after Haig to marry," Vartan began, "but it would mean an end to his adventuring days—." Then he caught himself, having realized what his comment suggested.

"That would not be a sacrifice for me if I were to find the right woman," Haig replied, growing more thoughtful as he continued. "There are more important things than roaming and adventuring and—and . . ."

"What might they be?" Anahid inquired of the stammering prince.

"Just what do you mean?" Vartan asked, as much for the prince as for himself.

"Are you answering my question with a question?" Anahid asked. "If you are, I can tell you that the man I marry must have a trade."

Vartan was aghast. "But Anahid, the prince will one day be the monarch of this land. What would he need with a trade?"

"Everyone should have a skill," Anahid insisted, "no matter who they are. In our village a skill is known as a Golden Bracelet. And to me this Golden Bracelet means much more than the gowns and jewels that wealth can provide. Wealth can be taken away, but a Golden Bracelet stays with its possessor forever."

Haig had fallen silent, and he was not aware until she was nearly out of sight that Anahid had filled her jug and silently departed their company. He could not think if she was right or not or if her demand was sensible or foolish. He knew only that, if he were to win her hand, he must do as she demanded.

The king and queen were troubled when they heard that their son had fallen in love with a simple peasant girl. But when they heard of the requirement she had made, their hearts were lifted, for they were sure their indolent, fun-loving son would not be capable of the discipline required to learn a craft.

But Haig was determined. "I will master a craft!" he exclaimed. "And when I have, I will marry Anahid."

To humor his son, the king sent out a decree to all the artisans in the country, that they meet to display their crafts before the prince. Having viewed all the handcrafts laid before him, Haig decided to learn the weaving of gold cloth. So the king arranged for the finest weaver in the land to instruct his son.

It wasn't long before Haig became a master weaver. He wove an exquisite cloth of gold for Anahid, and when she received it, she consented to marry him. As a token of her love, she entrusted the messenger with a return gift, a beautiful carpet that she had woven herself.

Anahid and Haig were soon married.

The king and queen came to love their son's bride for her good heart and her intelligence and, of course, for her own great weaving skills.

Years passed. The old king died, and Haig and Anahid ascended to the throne.

Then one day King Haig's dear friend and servant, Vartan, disappeared. For many months they sent out search parties looking for him. One party after another returned, without turning up a single clue. But King Haig and Queen Anahid would not give up, and together they made a plan. Haig would go out in disguise and inspect the country himself in order to find out why Vartan had vanished, while Anahid would quietly carry on the matters of state as if the king himself were present.

"I will return within a month's time," he told Anahid, "and if I do not, you can be sure that something has gone wrong."

Haig disguised himself as a peasant artisan and traveled throughout his kingdom in search of Vartan. He had come to learn of the sorcerer Zilnago, and he suspected that Vartan had come under his spell. One day while he was browsing in the bazaar of the same village where he had met Anahid, he stopped to finger the goods at one of the stalls. A merchant, taking him for a stranger, asked him who he was and where he came from.

Haig answered that he was a weaver of the finest gold cloth and that he came from a distant land, in search of work.

"I can use a man with such a skill," the merchant slyly remarked. "Follow me. My shop is but a short distance from here."

There was something about the man that caused Haig to become suspicious, but it seemed to him that he might obtain a lead if he were to pursue this opportunity.

He followed the merchant, who led him through several dark alleyways until they came to what appeared to Haig to be an abandoned building.

The man unlocked the door while Haig stood at his side anxiously peering into the dark entryway. When the door opened, the merchant shoved Haig inside and locked the door behind him. Then he called, "Supplies will be brought to you shortly, and then you will have your promised work."

Slowly Haig's eyes adjusted to the light inside. He soon realized he was in a dungeon and that all around him were other captives like himself. All of the prisoners were worn and emaciated, and many seemed close to death. As he peered at their forlorn faces, he suddenly recognized his faithful servant, Vartan, sitting in a corner, haggard and worn and dressed in rags.

They embraced at once, and then Vartan told him of the horrors of his captivity. The prison was run, he explained, by the sorcerer Zilnago and his followers. The prisoners were fed only bread and water and worked incessantly. If they were too slow or their work unsatisfactory, they were killed. Vartan began to sob when he realized that his very own king had been taken prisoner by the evil magician.

But Haig consoled him and said, "Take heart, my good and loyal friend. I will find a way to get us out of here."

At that moment, the door was flung open, and the sorcerer himself appeared. "So," he said to Haig, "you can weave cloth of gold."

"I will weave such a fabulous cloth of gold that its value will exceed half the wealth of this kingdom," Haig replied.

"If you are lying, you will regret it," Zilnago threatened.

"I am not lying," Haig answered, "but to do my work, I must have the appropriate materials."

"They will be here shortly," the sorcerer said, "and then we shall see."

It was soon evident to the sorcerer that Haig was a master craftsman. Vartan became Haig's assistant; working at his side, he kept the tension of the warp and weft. Haig demanded more food from the sorcerer both for himself and Vartan . . . to give them the strength they would need to quickly finish the golden cloth. The sorcerer was so impressed by Haig's work that he acceded to his demands, knowing that the faster the piece was completed, the sooner he would benefit from their labor.

Haig took strength from the beauty of the cloth he was weaving, as well as from the added provisions. Both he and Vartan grew stronger by the day. Although Haig worked with great speed, he wove an intricate cloth. In the upper right corner of the design, he created a Golden Bracelet, and inside the band he wove a hidden message with a map to show where he was being held captive.

When the cloth was finished, Haig suggested to the sorcerer that Queen Anahid, because of her weaving skills, would appreciate the worth of his piece. The sorcerer decided to take Haig's golden cloth to the queen himself.

During all this time, Anahid had carried on the king's duties with such expertise that no one realized that Haig was missing. But Anahid's nights were filled with worry. Her husband's return was overdue, and she had no idea where he was or what had become of him. Each day she grew more lonely, and she began to feel that she would perish if her beloved Haig did not soon return.

One day the sorcerer arrived in the guise of a merchant. He insisted upon seeing the queen herself. Anahid gave her consent and had him brought to her.

Anahid knew at once that she was in the presence of an evil man. But when she looked over the fabric he had brought, she saw immediately that it had been woven by Haig.

The queen looked up from the fabric, pretending to admire one who could show her such a work of art. "This is the most beautiful golden cloth that has ever been brought to this palace," she began. "I would like to meet the creator of this work. Bring him to me, for he should be rewarded for his efforts, as you, of course, will be rewarded for yours."

"But my gracious queen, I am afraid that would be impossible. The weaver resides in a land very far from here."

Anahid did not answer. She tried to calm herself and to conceal the fear that was in her heart. She was about to challenge the stranger and to demand the whereabouts of her husband when her eye fell upon the message inscribed inside the Golden Bracelet.

"You lie!" she shouted at once. "I know what you've done with my Haig." She turned and called out to her guards: "Take this man to the dungeon. He has captured our king. We must hurry and save him."

They put the sorcerer in chains, then hurriedly assembled a battalion of soldiers. Anahid herself led the search party, holding a tracing of the map that Haig had woven into the fabric.

When they arrived at the prison, they quickly broke down the door. The sorcerer's assistants were placed under arrest, and the captured slaves were saved. Haig and Vartan came out together, arm in arm, and Anahid ran to embrace them.

Vartan wept in gratitude. "Anahid, my good queen," he said, "you have saved us from a terrible fate."

"Yes," agreed the king, "but in truth you saved us many years ago when you told me that I should have a Golden Bracelet to protect me from my fate. I would not now be the king if I didn't have Anahid for my queen."

They rode home in procession, knowing they would rule wisely and well, with knowledge of their people, and with an undying devotion to one another, as well as for their sacred land.